ribbit

Jorey Hurley

A Paula Wiseman Book
Simon & Schuster Books for Young Readers
New York London Toronto Sydney New Delhi

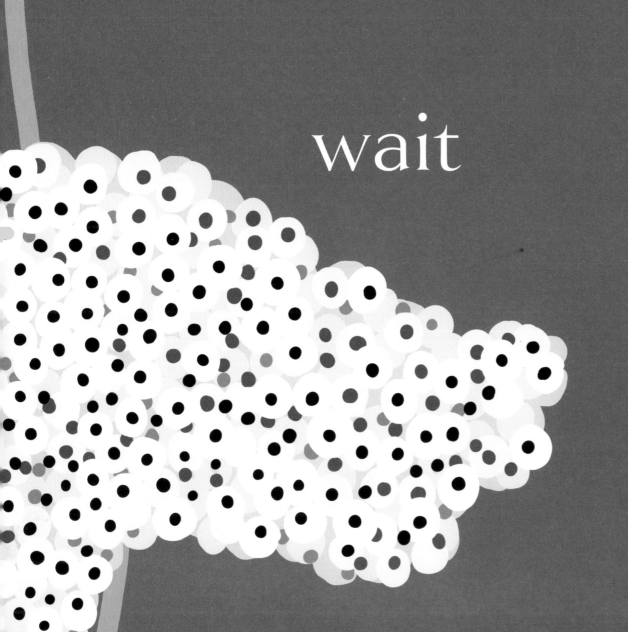

wait

hatch

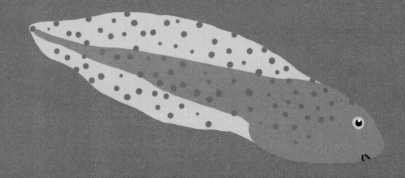

grow

change

climb

watch

catch

rest

leap

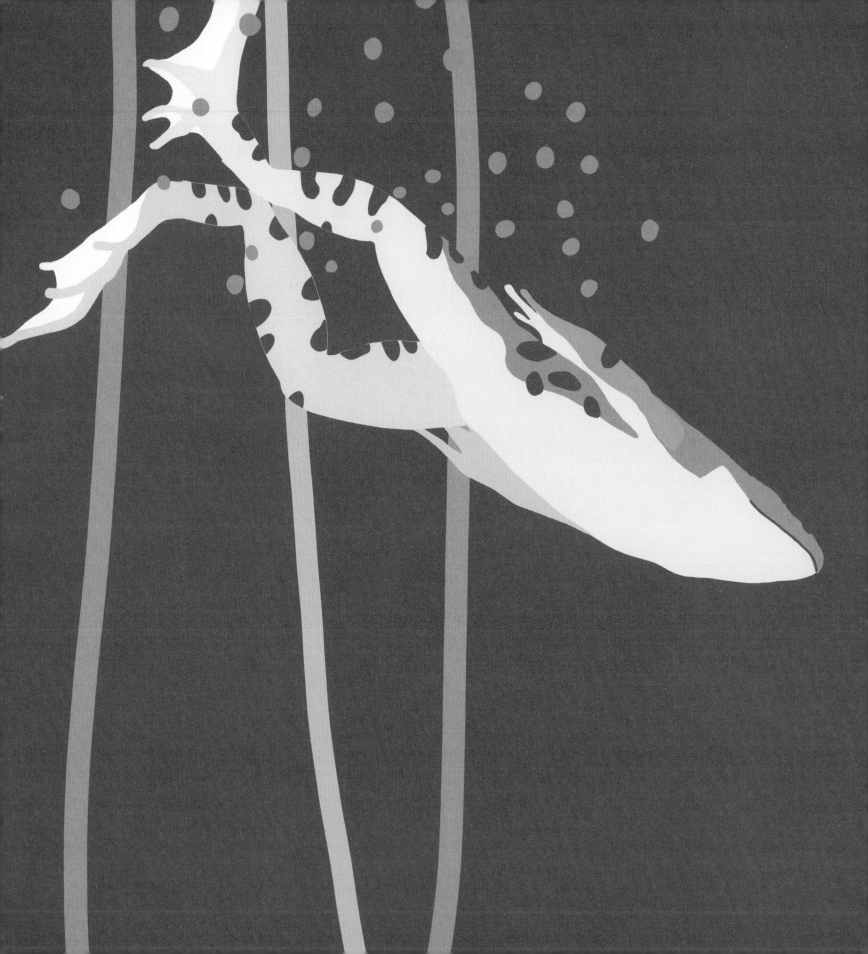

swim

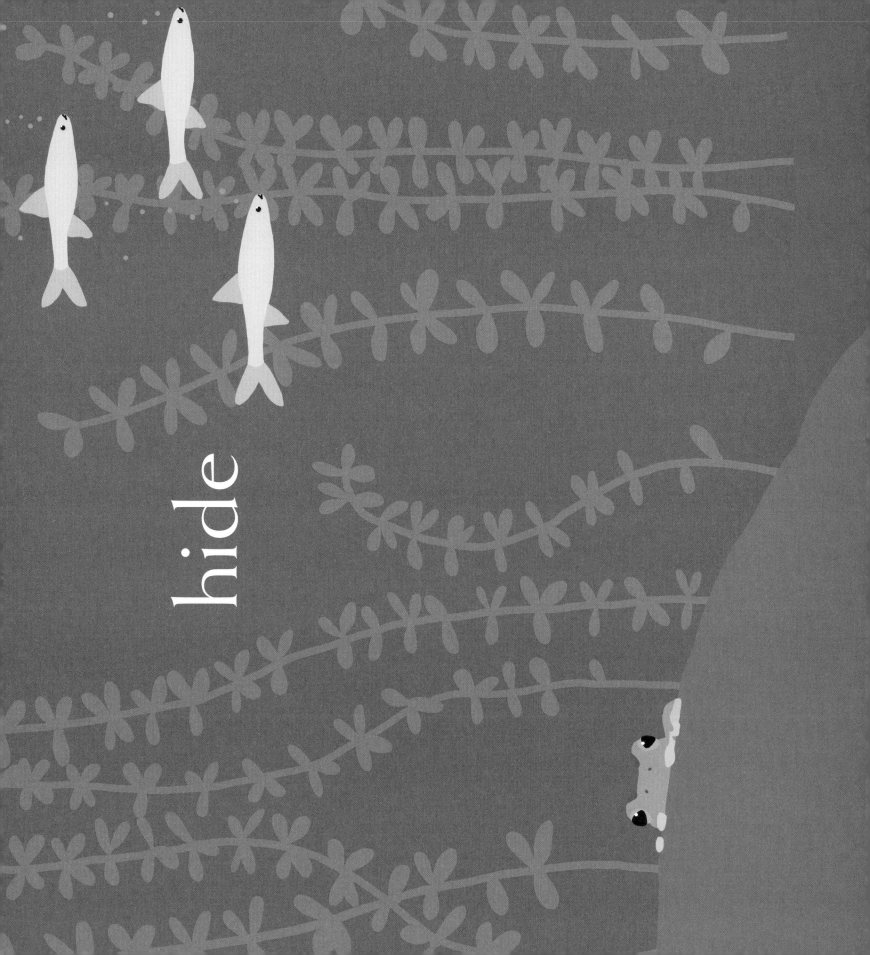

hide

hibernate

look

ribbit

wait

for Jon

SIMON & SCHUSTER BOOKS FOR YOUNG READERS • An imprint of Simon & Schuster Children's Publishing Division • 1230 Avenue of the Americas, New York, New York 10020 • Copyright © 2017 by Jorey Hurley • All rights reserved, including the right of reproduction in whole or in part in any form. • SIMON & SCHUSTER BOOKS FOR YOUNG READERS is a trademark of Simon & Schuster, Inc. • For information about special discounts for bulk purchases, please contact Simon & Schuster Special Sales at 1-866-506-1949 or business@simonandschuster.com. • The Simon & Schuster Speakers Bureau can bring authors to your live event. For more information or to book an event, contact the Simon & Schuster Speakers Bureau at 1-866-248-3049 or visit our website at www.simonspeakers.com. • Book design by Lizzy Bromley • The text for this book was set in Goldenbook. • The illustrations for this book were rendered in Photoshop. • Manufactured in China • 1116 SCP • First Edition • 10 9 8 7 6 5 4 3 2 1 • CIP data for this book is available from the Library of Congress. • ISBN 978-1-4814-3274-0 • ISBN 978-1-4814-3275-7 (eBook)

author's note

When I was a kid, my brother and I used to catch tadpoles and keep them in big buckets so we could watch them turn into frogs. It was irresistible to check on them every day and see who had grown legs and who had lost their tail. The frog in this book is a leopard frog. This frog, and others like it, are called "true frogs" because they all share similar body types (smooth and moist skin, powerful legs, and webbed feet) and habitats (near water). The toad and the tree frog are their close relatives, but they have important differences in either body type (toads have dry, bumpy skin and short legs) or habitat (tree frogs live primarily in trees).

True frogs live in freshwater, where their webbed feet help them swim. They need to keep their skin moist to stay alive, so they stay near water all the time. They live alone for most of the year, but they gather together in the springtime to breed and lay eggs. This is when you hear the most croaking, because male frogs croak to let other frogs know which territory is theirs and to attract females. They croak by sucking air into the "sac" under their mouth until it puffs out like a balloon. When they release the air from the sac, it makes their sound. Every kind of frog makes its own sound. Some croak, some grunt, some whistle, and some ribbit.

The females lay their eggs in the water, where the eggs stick together in clumps of thousands. After about a week, tadpoles hatch out of the eggs, ready to spend the summer growing and changing slowly into frogs. The tadpoles live entirely underwater, breathing through gills and eating algae and other tiny underwater plants. A lot of animals, such as insects and fish, like to eat them, but some tadpoles will survive. After a few weeks they begin to change into frogs. This change is called metamorphosis and starts with the growth of hind legs. Next the tadpole begins to grow lungs and will occasionally swim to the surface to take gulps of air. As the tadpole's lungs develop, its gills go away and it grows arms where the gills were. Once the tadpole is about three months old, its tail starts to shrink and it swims more and more with its webbed feet. After about two more weeks its tail will be completely gone and it will be ready to climb out of the water.

Young frogs are called froglets and look like small adult frogs. They need to eat as much as they can to grow bigger. Frogs are carnivores and will eat any mouth-size animal they can catch. Frogs hunt by sitting very still and waiting for an insect or other animal to come near. Then they flick out their long, sticky tongue and grab it. In addition to catching food for themselves, frogs need to avoid being eaten by predators. They have an advantage, because they can jump into the water to escape land-based predators (birds and snakes) and can jump back onto the land to escape aquatic predators (fish).

Frogs are cold-blooded, which doesn't actually mean that their blood is cold all the time. It means that their blood changes temperature depending on the temperature around them. When the air and water are warm, their blood warms up and they can move (and hunt for flies) quickly and easily. When the air and water are cold, their blood is cold and they can only move slowly or not at all, so frogs that live in places with cold winters will hibernate. They spend the winter asleep in the mud at the bottoms of ponds. Because they barely move during hibernation, they can absorb enough oxygen out of the water and don't need to swim up to the surface for air. When springtime warms the pond water, the frogs wake up from hibernation, hungry and ready to look for food.

Jonny Hurley